One cold December morning, Belle was in the castle stables, grooming Phillipe after a quick ride. As she brushed and brushed his golden mane, she thought of the coming holiday.

"Phillipe, remember how we used to celebrate Christmas? Papa, you, and I would go into the woods and find the best tree. Papa would chop it down, and you'd carry it home through the snow. Then we'd trim it with all our favorite ornaments, decorate the house, and cook a wonderful Christmas dinner. I'm going to miss that."

1

This Christmas, Belle was not going to be home with her father in their warm cottage. And the cold, dark castle that she shared with the Beast and the enchanted objects didn't have a gaily decorated tree or any signs of celebration. It looked like it was going to be a sad and lonely holiday.

Belle tried to stay hopeful. "Maybe the servants are planning something. I'll go find out."

Belle found Lumiere first. He was dancing with the Featherduster on tabletop. "Lumiere, does anyone in the castle celebrate Christmas?"

The friendly candelabra quickly stopped dancing. "Why no, cherie. The master, he is against it."

"Oh, Lumiere, it's Christmas. I think we should celebrate."

"Sacre Bleu! But the master's temper! I'm afraid it will never work."

3

Belle was determined to bring the Christmas spirit to the castle. The first thing she wanted to do was bake Christmas cookies and fill the whole castle with wonderful smells. She came upon Mrs. Potts, the teapot, in the kitchen.

"Oh, I'm so glad you're here, Mrs. Potts. I need your help. It's time to get ready for Christmas, and there's so much to do!"

Mrs. Potts was surprised. "Oh, my dear, that will never do. The master has forbidden any celebrating — especially at Christmas."

"Yes, I know." Belle was already looking through the cupboards. "But this Christmas is going to be different. This Christmas we're going to celebrate!"

Up in his room, the Beast heard laughter and chatter coming from downstairs. He came out into the hallway and saw Cogsworth, the mantel clock, hurrying by. "Cogsworth, what's going on?"

Cogsworth had heard about Belle's plans, but he didn't want to tell the Beast that Christmas was coming to the castle this year. "It appear that the young lady has taken it upon herself to ...bake ... something."

"But it sounds like everyone is in the kitchen with her."

"Ah, yes, that would seem a bit strange, wouldn't it? But the truth of he matter is, she likes the company. And everyone enjoys her company qually as much. Ah, if that will be all, Your Highness, I must be on my ay. I'm in charge of decorating … ah, cleaning the mantels."

The Beast could tell something was going on. "Hmm, I wonder …"

The Beast crept down the stairs and followed the sounds of laughter to the kitchen. There was Belle, working with the servants. The Stove had two steaming-hot pies sitting next to his burners and a tray of cookies browning in his oven. "Finally I get to do some real baking around here."

The Featherduster and Chip, the teacup, were making merry wreaths out of holly bushes and evergreen branches. Lumiere was trying to tie bright red bows onto the wreaths, but the flames on his

candles kept burning the ends of the ribbons. Mrs. Potts dashed madly around, trying to help everyone.

As the Beast turned to go, he moaned sadly. The servants stopped what they were doing and looked at Belle. She paused only for a moment, then continued rolling out cookie dough.

"It's all right, everyone. Once the decorations are up and the cookies are baked, he'll come around. Even a Beast can have the Christmas spirit — you'll see." The servants hoped Belle was right.

Late that night the Beast wandered through the castle, looking at the cheery decorations that the servants had put up. He was reminded of Christmases with his mother long ago. His eyes filled with tears, and he angrily tore the decorations down and stormed back to his room.

Unable to sleep, the Beast paced back and forth. "What should I do? What should I do?"

The next morning, Belle discovered the decorations all over the floor. Mrs. Potts was sitting on a tea cart nearby. "There, there, dear. It's a hard time for the master."

"Well, maybe if I gave him something special, he'd understand that Christmas is a time for sharing. Do you have any ideas?"

But Mrs. Potts was already on her way back to the kitchen. "I'm sure that whatever you give him will be lovely, my dear."

Belle sighed. "Maybe Lumiere will know."

Belle found Lumiere hanging mistletoe in the hallway. "Lumiere, what could I give Beast for Christmas?"

"Ah, let me think. Perhaps a handsome new tie would be nice."

"Oh, that's a good idea. Thank you." Belle didn't want to seem rude, but she was thinking more of something that would show him the spirit of Christmas. This was going to take a lot more work than she thought. She left to find Cogsworth.

Cogsworth was directing the servants as they decorated the library.

"Cogsworth, can you help me? I'm trying to think of a gift that would how Beast the true meaning of Christmas."

The picky mantel clock was delighted to be asked. "Well, perhaps a air of fuzzy slippers or a new robe."

Belle smiled politely. "Thank you, Cogsworth. That's very helpful."

As everyone was getting into the holiday spirit, the Beast stayed in his room more and more. Finally Mrs. Potts paid him a visit.

"You know, Master, it would be a lovely gesture if you gave Belle a Christmas gift. She's working so hard to cheer up the place — and you."

"What's the use? I wouldn't know where to begin."

"Just try, Master. It's Christmas, and I think a special gift from you would mean so much to her."

14

The Beast knew that Mrs. Potts was right. "Belle was happy when I gave her the library. What can I give her that will mean as much? Maybe I could make her something...."

He picked up a piece of wood and looked around his room. His eyes fell on the enchanted rose. "Well, maybe ..."

Meanwhile, Belle was in her room, feeling a bit low. She flopped down on her bed with a sigh. "What can I give Beast that would mean something to him, that would make him feel the joy of Christmas the way I do?"

The Wardrobe interrupted Belle. "Cheer up, dear. Why don't you pick out a pretty dress? You know, freshen up a bit? It always helped me when I was feeling blue."

Belle looked up at the Wardrobe. "But I need something for Beast, not for me."

"When you feel better, you think better. Come on, fling my doors open and take a peek."

Belle smiled at the Wardrobe. She slowly lifted the latch on the doors and gazed at the clothes inside.

Hanging among the beautiful gowns was the dress Belle had worn when she first arrived at the castle. She ran her fingers over the simple cloth and smiled at the wonderful memories it brought. Then she noticed that something heavy was in the pocket.

"Oh! Papa's gold watch! I'd forgotten that he left it here." Suddenly Belle had an idea. "Maybe someone else could use it."

While Belle was wrapping the Beast's gift, the Beast was madly trying to carve a beautiful rose for Belle. But his hands were too big and clumsy. "Who am I trying to fool? I can't make anything with these huge claws. I'm nothing but a monster to her."

The Beast threw the chunk of wood across the room. It hit an old dresser that he never used. A strange tinkling sound came from one of the drawers.

Slowly the Beast got up and walked over to the wobbly dresser. He yanked open the drawer and gasped at what he saw. "My mother's musical jewelry box!"

The finely carved wooden box had a tiny key. The Beast could turn it only a little, but it was enough to hear the melody of his mother's favorite song. Thoughts of Belle's kindness warmed him, and he knew he had found the right gift for her.

When Christmas Eve finally arrived, the castle had taken on Belle's warmth and cheeriness. There was a beautiful tree shining with candlelight and ornaments, and everyone looked forward to exchanging gifts. Especially Belle. "Do you think Beast will be coming down? I have something for him."

Mrs. Potts shook her head. "I wouldn't count on it, dear."

Still, Belle was hopeful.

"This is so much fun, Mama!" Chip was jumping up and down.
Cogsworth chimed in. "I'm rather wound up too."
Lumiere was also all aglow. "This old castle hasn't had this much excitement in ages."
Just then they heard the Beast plodding down the stairs. Everyone held their breath.

He had changed into his finest suit and was carrying a small gift-
wrapped box. Belle rushed up to him. "I … I wasn't sure you'd join us."

The Beast hesitated, then pushed the box into Belle's hands. "This
was my mother's. I'd like you to have it." He turned to go.

"Wait! I have something for you, too."

Belle handed him her gift. "It would mean so much to me if you'd
accept this. It...belonged to my father."

The Beast smiled at the gold watch. His mother's jewelry box would have been the perfect place to keep it. Belle was smiling too, thinking how handsome her father's watch would have looked in this beautiful jewelry box. Carefully she wound the key, then set the box on the mantelpiece. "I'll keep the box here so we can enjoy it together."

"And the watch will stay inside the box when I'm not using it. Then you can see it too. Merry Christmas, Belle."

Belle smiled warmly. "And a very merry Christmas to you, Beast."